RED VENOM
ATTACK!

Royston Drake

CARNIVAL

The image on the view screen was growing larger. Captain Buck Finn of the Manta Sharks and his opposite number, Captain Nigel Hunt of the Manta Wolves Terrain Force, leaned forward in their seats, trying to make out the shapes of unfamiliar continents on the blue and green orb that hung before them. "There she is," said Commander Quest, "New Earth!" The planet was half-covered by banks of drifting cloud, its surface wrinkled by mountain ranges through which tiny rivers ran. "That's at fifty-thousand magnification on the enhancer," their leader continued, squinting at the figures in the corner of the screen. He tapped the keys on his console and New Earth leapt away to become a pinprick of light amongst many others.

"What are the chances she'll be inhabited?" asked Captain Hunt.

"Strong," Quest replied, "though the likelihood that we'll find duplicate human beings at the same evolutionary level as ourselves is slight. In fact, it's one chance in —" he tapped the keyboard again and the resulting figure ran off the edge of the screen. "Er, let's just say the possibility is remote."

"Maybe they'll be in the middle of an Ice Age," Captain Finn said, "just like my home town, New Karelia."

Bill Quest and Captain Hunt exchanged a weary glance. Buck's Finnish jokes were wearing a little thin by this time. The Commander had programmed the Manta's computer to wake them from suspension at three random intervals in their journey. This was their third awakening, only hours after their bubbles had last been unravelled. Each time, Buck Finn came out with a variation on the same side-splitting observation about how cold it was in Finland, as though that was the only fact he'd managed to notice about his native country.

A green light flashed on the console and Bill Quest pressed viewspeak. It was most likely Sergeant Sweeney, reporting on the Viper Squad prisoners, as ordered. The three members of the Viper Squad had been captured during their attempt to sabotage the Manta Ship earlier in the mission. Sure enough, Sweeney's grizzled features flipped up onto the screen.

"They're pretty docile, sir," he said. "They must be the sorriest bunch of space-pirates I ever laid eyes on. Here, see for yourself, Commander." Sergeant Sweeney pressed a remote controller in his hand and the screen showed Ramon and the other two surviving stowaways, rubbing life back into their limbs, stretching their legs as best they could in the tiny cabin, designed as a punishment cell for one disobedient crew member. Then Ramon noticed that the camera high on the wall was following their movements. He approached, shaking his fist, gabbling silently on Bill Quest's screen.

"Let's hear what he's got to say, Sweeney," instructed the Commander and seconds later the sound of Ramon's voice faded up through the speaker:

". . . so, you think we're funny, eh, Commander high-and-mighty Quest? Well, I, Ramon Callisto, am here to tell you: you'll laugh on the other side of your face when Major Vex catches up with you. Then this new planet will be ours. We're tired of doing Earth's dirty work and living on dustbowl worlds – we want a home of our own. And we're going to get it!''

Bill Quest shook his head and cancelled the image on his screen, telling Sweeney to prepare the men for the final leg of their journey. He instructed the computer to complete the rest of the flight programme and soon the suspension bubbles cocooned the crew of Manta Force once again as the gigantic Command Ship tilted towards its final destination.

The Manta's retro-rockets flared in the blue darkness as the ship settled onto the surface of New Earth. Commander Quest had decided on a night-landing. The soft glow of instrument lights

in the command deck were all that might reveal something of the enormous shape of the interstellar craft to anyone who might be down there. No lights showing the outlines of cities had been visible from the upper atmosphere, not even fires that might indicate some kind of human settlement. The ship was touching down on the edge of a dense, luxuriant forest, of a kind that hadn't existed on Earth for many thousands of years. New Earth's largest ocean lapped at its fringes.

"Remember, men," said Bill Quest, addressing the entire crew through his throat microphone, "our instructions are to peacefully co-exist with the inhabitants of this planet, should there be any. I want you to remember that. We'll be sending out the first exploration teams at dawn. That means a lot of work between now, which we'll call –" he glanced at his chronometer "– 02.30 New Earth Time, and sun-up, when your commanding officers will be taking charge of the exploratory missions. That's all."

"Sir, aren't you forgetting something?" Nigel Hunt's voice piped up at his elbow.

"What?"

"My leg's still in plaster." The Manta Wolves Captain lifted up his right leg, which was itching furiously underneath the vinyl cast.

"Don't bother me now, Hunt. We've been in suspension; your leg's had years to heal. Now run down to Lieutenant Kaye in the sick bay and get that cast cut off."

Captain Hunt got up sheepishly and limped over to the descent tube. It was there that he had been injured during the battle with the Viper Squad saboteurs.

"And Hunt," Bill Quest called after him. "If there are any complications and he has to amputate, tell Lieutenant Kaye he has my permission to get an artiforg out of storage."

Captain Finn spluttered into his coffee, but Commander Quest silenced him with a sharp look. The big Scandinavian gulped down a final mouthful of the disgusting brew and stood up. It was time to get the Manta Sharks Navy into gear. He followed Captain Hunt towards the descent tube.

The sky grew lighter over the forest and the sounds of birdsong and screeching small animals began to build up slowly, as though someone had their

finger on a hidden volume control. The Manta Attack Ship had been raised on its hydraulic rams and the crews of the Manta Wolves, Sharks and Hawks were standing by for their final instructions.

The Gundog and the Strike Bike, which had both been damaged in the struggle with the Viper Squad stowaways, had undergone repairs during the flight. But there had been no opportunity to test the overhauled motors in the confined space of the Manta's lower deck. Now Captain Hunt ordered the Manta Wolves mechanics to start them up and test drive the two vehicles along the wide sandy beach.

Corporal Scott Ramsey pressed the start button and the Strike Bike shrieked into life. He was looking forward to putting the machine through its paces. Behind him Private "Chubby" Rake was warming the Gundog's rebuilt four litre engine. Ramsey waved "Chubby" Rake ahead. He'd give him a good start along the empty beach, then overtake on the more powerful turbo-charged Strike Bike.

The two Manta Wolves Terrain Vehicles were neck and neck when the calm surface of the ocean was broken by a sudden boiling turbulence. Ramsey was on the land-side, all his attention focused on overtaking Private Rake's Gundog. His task was made easier when the other driver shut back suddenly and coasted to a halt. Ramsey glanced in his offside wing mirror. "Chubby" Rake was no longer driving. He was looking out to sea, gaping open-mouthed, then scrabbling around to man the Gundog's rear-mounted gun.

A head had appeared above the waves, about fifty metres out, a monstrous head from which a huge crest of bone protruded. The creature opened its mighty jaws and let out a roar, raising its head towards the clear blue sky. Then it continued to wade ashore.

The Strike Bike threw up a great sheet of sand as Corporal Ramsey swung around to race back towards the Gundog. "Strewth!" gasped Scott as more of the creature became visible. "It's a giant kangaroo!" But he was wrong. The monster was a Parasaurolophus. On Earth such animals had been extinct for 130 million years. Here, at least one example had survived. And he was angry.

Panicking, "Chubby" let loose a hail of fire from the Gundog's artillery. One or two of the laser shells found their mark, but failed to penetrate the thick hide of the Parasaurolophus, enraging the enormous beast even further. As Scott skidded to a halt beside the Gundog his helmet radio crackled into life.

"Don't kill the animal," Captain Hunt's voice

rapped tinnily in his ear. "We want to study the creatures of this planet, not exterminate them!"

"Yes, sir," said Corporal Ramsey, though he wasn't too happy with the order. It was all very well for Captain Hunt – he was watching at a safe distance back at the Command Base. Nevertheless, Rake and Ramsey set their weapons on stun and fired together, pummelling the monster's thick hide with bolts of energy that would've been powerful enough to stop an elephant. The Parasaurolophus merely flicked its massive head in annoyance.

At that moment a great shadow blotted out the sun. Scott Ramsey looked up and saw a giant shape wheeling in the sky, diving at the Manta Command Base. It seemed that another of New Earth's creatures had been woken up by their noisy new neighbours – and now the Command Base had problems of its own.

"It's – it's a flying lizard," stammered Captain Hunt, "and the brute's diving straight for us!"

"Good Lord!" Bill Quest muttered. "I do believe we have a visitor. And if I'm not mistaken that creature is a Quetzalcoatlus, an airborne killer-lizard named after the Aztec god of Earth's ancient history. Look at the size of it!"

"With the greatest respect, sir, can we save the anthropology lesson for later?" Captain Finn asked.

But Commander Quest was already in full control of the situation. He sprinted over and jumped into the cockpit of Blue Lightning, the one man jet fighter whose designers claimed to be the fastest strike plane ever built. "Finn," he barked, "take the Aquattack and approach the Parasaurolophus from the rear. I think the Manta Wolves are in trouble.'

Within seconds Quest was in the air, but by that time the giant lizard had already landed. While the troops ran for cover inside the Manta's hull, the Quetzalcoatlus perched on the edge of the Command Module, beating the air with its huge leathery wings, slashing at the men who cowered inside with its powerful tail as they opened fire with their puny hand-lasers. "SKRAAKKK!" the lizard cried, snapping its jaws against the ship's heavily armoured hull, turning to flick its bullwhip tongue into the Manta's interior, hoping to catch a tasty breakfast morsel.

"We can't hold out much longer," Captain Hunt said, instructing the Manta troops to aim into the creature's mouth. "If only we could get the Battle Copter airborne we might have a chance."

He had reckoned without Commander Quest's mastery of the Blue Lightning fighter. Screaming from the sky, their leader raked the lizard's back with laser fire. "KREEEKK!" The animal let out a howl of pain and shot into the air, giving chase to the annoying blue creature that had dared to attack it. Ultra-manoeuvrable, the little fighter drew the Quetzalcoatlus out over the sea, flipping over in a tight circle to fire again into the lizard's belly.

Bill Quest had no desire to harm the creature, merely to frighten it away. Like poor Corporal Ramsey and Private Rake, still trying to hold off the other dinosaur from the beach, his guns were set on stun. To his surprise and relief the plan seemed

to have worked. The lizard dived down low, and flying close to the ocean, fled towards the safety of the distant mountains which rose behind the forest. Somewhere in its tiny brain, the Quetzalcoatlus made a mental note to be more cautious in future.

Far below, Captain Finn had astonished the Parasaurolophus by executing a series of high speed runs at the animal, each time missing him by inches. Bill Quest watched with amusement as the Aquattack kicked up a wide arc of spray, swerving away at the last moment to drench the unfortunate dinosaur. Pretty soon the Parasaurolophus got the message and, half-submerging its ungainly body, lumbered along parallel to the beach, hoping to wade ashore in peace by the swampy mouth of a river further up the coast.

At least we now know where New Earth is on the evolutionary scale, thought the Commander as he headed back to the Manta Command Base. *We don't have to worry about meeting any other human beings – we're 120 million years too early.*

He brought the Blue Lightning in to a perfect three-point landing beside the loading ramp. It seemed to Commander Quest that a slight change of plan was necessary.

He found the men in jubilant mood, eager to refuel the vehicles and set out on further exploration. Calling Captain Finn and Captain Hunt aside, Quest explained that they must concentrate instead on establishing a base – and setting up the more powerful transmitter needed to make Vid-link contact with Earth. "We just can't be sure they won't come back, gentlemen," he concluded, slapping his regulation gold gloves into an open hand. "We've simply got to protect ourselves."

Ramon and the other Vippie prisoners were soon set to work, helping to unload the ship, while practised teams in yellow, blue and white uniforms erected storage and sleeping bubbles in the shadow of the huge mother ship. After an hour's solid work, the generator whirred into life and the huge Vid-link screen flickered and cleared. Commander William Julius Quest prepared to make the historic announcement that Manta Force had arrived on New Earth.

"You're doing a great job, Bill," said President Bataille, gesturing warmly towards the Vid-Cam. "I'm sure I speak for all Earth's suffering, hoping people when I say: Good luck, Manta Force, and God bless you. Our hearts are out there with you, beyond the stars."

"Er, thanks Mr President." Commander Quest was distinctly rattled. He hadn't expected to be on prime time TV as soon as they made contact, watched by the masses of Earth, lying on their bunks in the vast dormitories. Manta Force must be good for Jim Bataille's popularity rating. The success of the mission would probably mean an early election and a further fifteen years in office for Bill Quest's childhood friend.

"Now I want to show you and the brave men of Manta Force a little surprise we've got ready for you," President Bataille continued. At that point the Vid-Cam pulled back and the TV audience, including the men on New Earth, saw that he was broadcasting live from Cape Jackson, surrounded by scientists and civil servants. They were seated on a stage in front of a hangar, from which a sleek red fighting machine was taxi-ing. "Commander Quest, ladies and gentlemen, I give you . . . Red Venom!" The dignitaries broke into a vigorous round of applause and Bataille's face split open in a wide, sincere smile.

Gathered around the Vid-screen on New Earth, the Manta Force troops cheered, relieved that reinforcements would soon be on the way. Bill Quest was impressed by the new spaceship too, but he wished the President hadn't chosen to announce it in this flamboyant way. There were other matters to be discussed, which could not be raised while half the world was listening in. The Vippie stowaways had failed, but Bataille must be warned that they would try again. Or perhaps the President himself had some further news of Major Vex . . .?

". . . Red Venom is a heavily-armed, deep space

fighter, with independent fighting pods mounted in its wings," Jim Bataille went on, while a 3D graphic rotated on the Vid-screen, exploding to show Red Venom's various components. "In addition, Red Venom carries the Trojan personnel carrier and rocket launcher *and* the Hoverfly land and air scout vehicle . . . both of which can combine to form a single, all-purpose vehicle."

Commander Quest was beginning to feel like a contestant who has just been shown tonight's star prize on a TV game show. He half-expected Earth's supreme ruler to pull out a stack of little cards and start asking him questions about the Vid-stars of yesteryear.

But now the screen was given over to shots of Red Venom's take-off. The huge interstellar fighter with its raked-back wing formation rose into the air almost too fast for the Vid-Cam to track. It was an impressive, almost frightening sight. "Red Venom will now commence its proving trials," the President concluded. "After which it will cross the galaxy to join Commander Quest's heroic Manta Force on New Earth. Okay Bill. Over to you."

The Commander realised, uneasily, that he was on the air. "I'll look forward to its arrival, Mr President. Red Venom will be a valuable addition to our forces here on New Earth. However, there is one matter I'd like to –" But the Vid-Link chose that moment to develop a technical fault. The image on the Vid-screen broke up into jagged lines and the President's voice was drowned out by howling static. Suddenly the screen went dark altogether.

"It's no good, Commander," the technician explained, "we can't maintain that level of power for longer than a few minutes."

"Never mind," said Quest. "We've got plenty to do." It would be many months before Red Venom arrived. In the meantime they had to map out New Earth's continents from the lower atmosphere and create a secure base from which to carry out land and sea exploration. Dinosaurs or no dinosaurs.

Red Venom test pilots Rip Foster and Dewey Sandhurst were nearing the end of the first phase of their trial. In order to test the top speed of the space-fighter they had flipped out through the solar system in maximum hyper-drive. And to test the new ship's manoeuvrability, they had programmed a number of hyper-speed zig-zags between the nearest planets.

"She sure handles well," said Rip admiringly, "flips in and out of hyper-drive like a two-speed razor."

Dewey nodded in smiling agreement. This was the kind of assignment that made his job worthwhile. And, maybe, just maybe, he would later be picked from the pool to actually fly this crate out to join Commander Quest and Manta Force. He frowned suddenly. "Wait a minute, I'm picking something up in the headphones – a strong signal. What do you make of it?"

Rip flicked on his helmet radio. "Yes, I can hear it too. A distress signal. Where are we?" As if to answer his own question he pulled Red Venom out of hyper-drive, trying to get a fix on the radio signal. The great rings of Saturn clicked into view, turning majestically below them. "It's coming from the far side of Saturn." He turned to Dewey Sandhurst. "It's our duty to respond," he said, "proving flight or not."

"Right, skipper," said Dewey. "Let's see how fast we can get there!"

Life on Earth Relay 3 was pretty boring most of the time. It wasn't often that Freddie Drone got to do anything important, like tracking Red Venom on its first flight. Usually he just listened to his collection of classic digital tapes and drank too much non-

alcoholic beer. Or if he was really desperate he'd
hook up to one of the Vid-link Talk-Ins they ran for
workers in unsocial occupations. Trouble was,
after two years on Earth Relay 3, he didn't really
have much to say. Watching Red Venom was fun,
even though the ship was no more than a wildly
jumping bleep on his radar screen.

Then the bleep wasn't there any more. Surely,
there must be some . . . Freddie held the
headphones to his ear and punched in a direct
radio link at Red Venom's frequency. "Come on
you guys," he said. "I know you're out there.
Stop fooling around." In his ear he heard nothing
but the broken-up whistling of deep space and
snatches of interference from far-off satellites. The
interstellar fighter had simply blinked out of

existence. Nervously, Freddie punched in Earth-control at Cape Jackson. They weren't going to be very pleased with him.

The Manta ship was locked in a mapping orbit in New Earth's upper atmosphere. The ship's scanners were so sensitive that one complete sweep over a newly colonized world would provide all the geography they'd ever need, even down to the number of trees on a particular hillside.

Buck Finn was bored rigid. He stared out sourly at the great curve of New Earth's horizon. At the moment they were flying in the night-half of the planet, but in fifteen minutes they would burst into the brilliant, unshielded sunlight . . . again.

"Penny for your thought, Captain Finn," said Commander Quest, who was taking this opportunity to bring the ship's log up to date.

"I've got more than one thought in my head!" Buck protested.

"In that case, Finn, you've got one to spare. Why not share it with us? I'll even record your words in the ship's log, where your grandchildren will be able to read them."

Captain Finn cleared his throat and began gravely. "To my grandchildren," he said, "I leave the following advice: 'Stay out of the Navy if you don't like getting wet.' It's a proverb, taught to me by my mother."

Commander Quest snapped off the voc-scribe in annoyance. He was about to give Finn a short lecture on the seriousness of the ship's records when Captain Hunt's voice broke in.

"There's something big showing up, just over the horizon," said the Manta Wolves leader urgently, pointing at a fast-moving shape on the forward view-screen. "It's about the size of a small asteroid; coming in from out of system."

"Perhaps it *is* a small asteroid," said Commander Quest.

"We'll be able to see for ourselves in 30 seconds from now," Captain Finn pointed out. "We're about to do some more sun-bathing."

The Manta broke through into the sunlight moments later, and the sight that greeted them brought immediate hushed amazement. Screaming towards them out of the sun, its unmistakeable red livery bathed in fire, was Red Venom. "B-But they're not due here for months," protested Captain Hunt, gesturing helplessly towards the interstellar fighter that just shouldn't be there.

"Something's wrong, Commander," Captain Finn cut in. "I can't raise them on any of the com-link frequencies. Doesn't seem to be anything wrong with their signal; they're just not answering."

"That's because we're under attack," Quest said coolly. "Sound immediate combat alert. Gentlemen, I believe we have a fight on our hands."

The Commander of Manta Force had never spoken a truer word. The fighting machine that hurtled towards them with intent to reprocess the Manta into space-junk had been designed with a strike capability to complement that of the first Manta ship. Red Venom was faster than the fully-loaded Command Base; it was also far more heavily armed. Quest realised that they couldn't hope to outmanoeuvre their sister-ship. The only way was to wait until they could see the yellows of Red Venom's eyes, and then to blast the attacker with everything they had.

The tension was unbearable throughout the ship as Captain Hunt sat forward at his console, his fingers poised above the buttons that would send the Manta's missiles streaking towards their target. On the lower deck the combat alert siren was still sounding. The whole crew was on standby, strapped helplessly into their seats. In the ship's punishment cell the Vippie prisoners had also heard the alarm. They sat silent and still on the bunk, listening intently, half-hopeful, half-afraid.

In the last desperate minute before the point of no return the Vid-link screen on the command console cleared and Bill Quest was face to face with his adversary. It was the man that President Bataille had described as the most dangerous extremist in the galaxy: Major Leon Vex, leader of the Viper Squad. His features were arrogant, hard. A dark moustache was slashed across his upper lip, concealing a mouth that was twisted in amusement.

"Good morning, Commander. I haven't much to say, so I'll make it short and to the point. You are a worthless lackey of the most corrupt President in your planet's miserable history. And now you are going to die. Farewell, Quest. The rightful inheritors of New Earth will celebrate this moment forever."

Somehow Vex had jammed his broadcast into all the Manta's vid-screens. His defiant words echoed around the ship (the Vippie prisoners cheered weakly) and then the screens went dead. On the command deck Bill Quest fired both the Manta's guided missiles in quick succession. "Okay, Finn. Now get us out of here."

The exchange was over in a matter of seconds. Red Venom's deadly rocket-launchers had discharged at the same moment as the Manta weapons; now both ships veered in opposite directions, racing away from an explosion that overtook them as two of the missiles collided in mid-flight. The huge Manta Command Ship was tossed upwards like a leaf caught in a gust of wind. Commander Quest switched to manual and wrestled for control as the blinding flash bathed everything in white light.

For a moment Buck Finn thought he was on his way to heaven, then he realised that the Manta was still in one piece. On the console in front of him half-a-dozen red lights were flashing angry damage reports. He made a rapid estimate of how badly they were hit. "It's no good, Commander," he said almost immediately. "We've got to get down, quickly. Otherwise we're finished."

"Any sign of Red Venom?" asked Quest. Then he caught sight of the enemy ship himself, moving high and fast, trailing a white flare of burning metal from one wing tip.

"She's hit!" Captain Hunt exclaimed. "Looks like she might break-up at any moment."

"So might we," said Quest. "We've got to get back to base immediately. Red Venom may be wounded, but she's still dangerous. If Major Vex catches us in this condition, he'll finish us off. Down on the surface we can deploy the other Manta Force vehicles. Major Vex may be an excellent pilot, but these Viper Squad rebels will be no match for the Manta Wolves and the Manta Sharks. Not to mention the Hawks. I know of at least one Blue Lightning pilot that would love to wipe that arrogant smile off Leon Vex's face."

Limping badly, the Manta made it back to base with only one of her hyperboost engines

operational. As the great ship settled, Bill Quest and the others scanned the skies of New Earth for signs of Red Venum.

"There she goes," said Captain Finn, following a streak of fire like a falling star with his outstretched finger. "She's coming down on the other side of the bay, about thirty kilometres away. That's if she makes it at all."

There was no time to waste. Once again the Command Base loading doors swung open and the hydraulic rams hissed as the Manta Attack Ship was raised. "Deploy Manta Hawks . . . Deploy Manta Sharks . . . Deploy Manta Wolves . . ." The orders boomed from the speakers in the Command Base, echoing in the helmet radio of every Manta Force crew member. The two-man Hydro-Blaster skimmed out into the bay, while the Aquattack submarine dived beneath the clear blue waters and the S.A.M. waded after it. The Rocket-Rammer churned up the coast and suddenly the sky of New Earth was filled with howling Assault aircraft.

"Fix me up another Com-link with Quest," said Leon Vex quietly to one of his Viper Squad lieutenants. "Ah, Commander," he continued smoothly when his enemy's face appeared on the vid-screen, "I see you are still with us – for the time being. We've decided to give you one chance to save your wretched skin. Surrender to me at once and you will be permitted to live. You have three seconds to decide. One . . . two . . . three . . ."

"Manta Force doesn't surrender to crackpot space-pirates," snapped Quest. "Or to anyone else for that matter. Do your worst, Vex. Manta Force is more than a match for your deluded visions of conquest."

Angrily, Major Vex wrenched the cables from the back of his personal vid-link. "There will be no more talking," he rasped. "Deploy Red Venom Forces. Wipe Quest off the face of New Earth. Now is the moment to capture this new world for the hungry colonists of Saturn, Jupiter and Callisto."

The Trojan personnel carrier, loaded down with Viper Squad troops, was already detaching itself from Red Venom's central section. The heavy-tracked vehicle ground away towards the swampy shoreline, the Hoverfly rising from its back like a poisonous insect, skimming out across the placid

ocean to intercept the approaching Manta Battle Copter. One by one the four manned pods shot from the fighting ship's wings. The Skypod rose to protect the rear of the darting Hoverfly. The Aquapod dived into the ocean. The two-man Molepod leapt a short distance into the air, then buried itself in the ground, its corkscrew rotor burrowing under the forest – towards the unguarded rear of the Manta Command Base.

In their cramped prison cabin on the Manta, one of the captured Vippies had brought out the compressed-air space-knife, made in the underground workshops of Saturn, from a hiding place that had been missed by their captors. Now that everyone was too busy to guard them, Ramon used the powerful blade to smash open the casing of the holo-lock that secured the door. Then they would steal quietly through the deserted ship and make their way up to the command module. No compromise was possible. The battle to decide who controlled New Earth had already begun.